Robert
and the
Lemming
Problem

by Barbara Seuling
Illustrated by Paul Brewer

Cricket Books
Chicago

Library of Congress Cataloging-in-Publication Data

Seuling, Barbara.
   Robert and the lemming problem / by Barbara Seuling ; illustrated by
Paul Brewer.— 1st ed.
      p. cm.
Summary: Robert's teacher wants everyone in the class to try something
new, so Robert tastes asparagus and learns to play the tuba before
finding the perfect thing.
   ISBN 0-8126-2686-9 (cloth : alk. paper)
   [1. Schools—Fiction. 2. Individuality—Fiction. 3. Family
life—Fiction.] I. Brewer, Paul, 1950- ill. II. Title.
   PZ7.S5135 Rp 2003
   [Fic]—dc21
                                                    2002151415

For Barbara Buoncristiano
We go way back and we're still laughing—
how bad is that?
—B. S.

For Debby Vetter and Paula Morrow.
—P. B.

Contents

The Uncool Sneakers

Robert thumped upstairs to his room. He flopped into his beanbag chair, yanked off his new sneakers, and threw them across the room. Flo and Billie, his two turtledoves, flapped around in their cage.

All day long, Jesse Meiner had made fun of Robert's new sneakers. "They're so uncool," he said. "Get with it, Robert. Everyone who's cool wears High Jumps."

Robert didn't care if he was cool or not. What difference did it make if he wore his sneakers or High Jumps?

Robert would love to talk to his mom about it. She could always make him feel better. She would say something like, "It's just a lot of silly talk, Rob. Your sneakers are fine." But his mom was at her office on Tuesdays.

Sometimes he could talk to his brother, Charlie, but Charlie liked to tease him, and that's the last thing he needed right now. Besides, Charlie had hockey practice after school, and then he'd probably study with his friend Chris. They were studying the Middle Ages, when battles were fought on horseback and soldiers wore armor and carried banners to show whose army they were in. That's all Charlie talked about these days.

Robert's dad would be home soon. He was a teacher and left school at three o'clock, just like Robert. His dad was harder to talk to. He always liked to make lessons out of problems. Robert wasn't in the mood for a lesson. He had already talked to Paul Felcher, his best friend, on the way home from school. He would just have to wait for his mom to come home.

Robert got up and went to see how his animals were. The birds had calmed down, now that Robert had stopped throwing his shoes around. He opened their cage and let them out for a little exercise.

"Hello, Fuzzy," he said to his pet tarantula. He opened the tank to talk to her. He still didn't handle her much, but he was getting better at it. He was happy just to have her company and to feed her a cricket or two every week.

Tomorrow was Author Day at school. Robert had been looking forward to this day for a long time. Frank Farraday was coming. He was the author of a gazillion books, all about wildlife. That was right up

Robert's alley. He loved animals of all kinds.

Robert filled the little cup in the bird-cage with bird food. He refilled the water cup in the bathroom and went back to his room.

"Come on, Flo. Come on, Billie." Robert coaxed the birds down from the curtain rod and onto his arm, then into the cage.

Robert had been thrilled when Mrs. Bernthal chose him to be Frank Farraday's host. That meant he would show the author around and escort him from room to room. But what if Frank Farraday noticed that Robert's sneakers were not High Jumps? Would he care? Would it matter? How could Robert look uncool in front of Frank Farraday?

He had to get his mind off his sneakers. He had a report due on Friday. It had to be about something in the world he didn't like and what he would do to fix it. He dumped his book bag on his bed and took out his notebook and pencil. He sat at his desk and opened the notebook to a new page.

He thought about things he didn't like. Liver. Math. He couldn't write about them.

There would always be liver and math because they were good for you. He just didn't like them.

People making fun of other people really bothered him. What would he do about that? Catch the person and make him apologize. And buy a present for the person that he made fun of so that person would feel better. He tapped his pencil. That was pretty lame.

Smoking. He really hated smoking. It made you look ugly to smoke, and it polluted your lungs and gave you cancer. Once, he and Paul tried to stop people on the street from smoking. His class had just seen a movie about how bad smoking was for you. The people they stopped told them to go away and kept on smoking anyway.

He thought about animals that were treated badly. Robert once saw a picture in a magazine of a fox that had been caught in a steel trap. The fox had chewed its own paw off to get free. Robert's stomach flipped when he thought about it. That would be too hard to write about. He'd better choose something else. But what?

He put his pencil down. He had not written one word. He went downstairs with a soft *thump, thump* to get something to eat. He opened the refrigerator and took out the container of milk. He smelled it. His mom was so busy, she didn't always remember to replace the milk before it went sour.

Good. It was fine. He poured a tall glassful and then found some chocolate-covered jelly cookies to go with it.

It was amazing how cookies and milk always made him feel better. He hadn't thought about sneakers for at least ten minutes.

No Help

As he licked the chocolate coating off a cookie, Robert heard the car in the driveway. Sure enough, the clock on the kitchen wall said it was 3:42 exactly, the time his dad drove into the driveway every day. Robert heard the squeal of the garage door opening and closing and the car door slamming.

"Hi, Tiger," said Robert's dad, coming into the kitchen from the garage entrance.

"Hi, Dad."

"What's cooking?"

"Nothing," said Robert.

"Really?" His dad put his briefcase on the table and helped himself to a juice drink from the refrigerator. "That was your day? Nothing?"

"Well . . ."

"What is it, Tiger? You look worried." He sat down.

"Dad, all the kids are wearing the same kind of sneakers in school. They're called High Jumps."

"And?"

"And my sneakers are not that kind."

"Well, Robert. Didn't your mother just get you those sneakers?"

"Yes, but . . ."

"Well, money doesn't grow on trees, Robert," his dad said with a smile. "We can't get you a new pair of sneakers just so you can be like your friends."

"No, Dad, I . . ."

10

"Your new sneakers don't hurt your feet, do they?"

"Oh no. It's not . . ."

"Well, then it would be a waste of money to get another pair for no good reason. Isn't that true?"

11

"Yes, that's what I . . ."

"Of course. That's right. Wear the sneakers you have and be happy with them. I'm sure your mother would say the same thing." His dad got up and picked up his briefcase. "I'll be in my study grading papers if you need me for anything," he said.

How did that happen? Robert wondered, watching his father leave the kitchen. I didn't want to buy new sneakers. I just wanted to figure out how to stop the kids from teasing me. He never even heard my problem, but he thinks he fixed it!

He just had to face this sneakers thing on his own. Grownups were no help.

The Author

Robert took the school bus. He decided to wear his hiking boots from last year, which were a bit too small. His toes felt like they were in jail. He didn't think they would feel any better walking four blocks to school.

When the bus stopped at Paul's corner, Robert opened the window. "Get on the bus, Paul!" he shouted, waving his arm to catch Paul's attention. Paul got on and sat next to Robert.

"How come we're riding?" asked Paul.

They usually walked in good weather so they had more time to talk.

"My boots are tight. I don't think I can walk too far in them."

"So why are you wearing tight boots?" asked Paul. "I thought you just got new sneakers."

"Well," said Robert, "because of Frank Farraday." Robert looked embarrassed. "I don't want him to think I'm uncool."

"Uncool?" said Paul, frowning. "Don't listen to Jesse and the other kids. You're one of the coolest people I know. You have a tarantula for a pet, don't you?"

Paul always knew what to say to make Robert feel better.

"I guess," Robert said. "I was dumb for letting Jesse bother me. But it's too late now." He tried to wiggle his toes and couldn't.

"It's only for today," said Paul.

The minute Robert got into his classroom, he checked everything. All the books by Frank Farraday were on display around the room. A big poster, painted by Paul, the best artist in the class, hung on the door.

Around the edges of the poster were pictures of books with titles printed on them. *Wildlife Rescue. A Bird's Life. Coyotes in the Backyard. Return of the Wolves. Animal Feet. Bringing Back the Buffalo. Gorilla Baby. In Search of Humpback Whales.* Frank Farraday had written lots more, but those were the ones they had in their class library.

Jesse walked up to Robert. His eyes went right to the hiking boots. "Those are cool—" Robert felt his heart jump "—if you're in the country," said Jesse. "What is it with you? Get in step, man!"

"Going hiking, Robert?" asked Joey Rizzo. Abby Ranko and Melissa Thurm giggled. Robert could not think about that now. He went up to Mrs. Bernthal's desk.

"Mrs. Bernthal, may I borrow a pitcher from the teachers' lounge? Mr. Farraday might like a drink of water."

"Yes, you may, Robert. That's a very good idea," said Mrs. Bernthal.

Robert left the room. In the teachers' lounge he took a big plastic pitcher and let the water run into it while he searched for a cup. He returned to his classroom with the pitcher sloshing over with water. Stuffed in his shirt pocket was a plastic cup.

"Oh, dear," said Mrs. Bernthal, moving papers to make room on her desk. Robert put the pitcher down without spilling a drop. He put the plastic cup next to the pitcher.

Robert fidgeted in his seat. He was wearing his favorite green shirt, which was always fine, but today it made him itch. His toes were hot. If only he could take his boots off for a while.

The class was supposed to be following the instructions on pages four and five of their math workbooks. Robert couldn't help looking at the folder he had made to give to the author. FRANK FARRADAY, AUTHOR was spelled out across the front cover in colored markers. Every other letter was green. The letters in between were black. It really looked nice. Inside the folder, several pages of facts about the author's books had been stapled.

"All right, class. Let's go around the room. Andrew, what's the answer to number one?"

Andrew Liskin answered quickly. "Seventy-eight." Of course it was correct. Andy was a whiz at math.

Matt Blakey was next. Mrs. Bernthal continued around the room until she got to Robert. "Robert, what is the answer to number seven?"

"I didn't get that one," he replied.

"Did you get the one before it?"

"Um, no."

"Which ones did you get?"

"I . . . I didn't get any," Robert replied, staring at the empty pages in front of him.

"Well, you can add that to your homework tonight," said Mrs. Bernthal. "I know you're excited about Frank Farraday's visit. We all are. But that doesn't excuse you from doing your classwork."

Robert felt his cheeks get hot as Mrs. Bernthal went on to Susanne Lee Rodgers.

Extra homework. He would have to work hard to get all his homework done by eight o'clock. Otherwise, he would not be allowed to watch *The Instant Millionaire*. Robert and Paul watched the program every week to see how much money they would win if they were on the show. Paul once got up to $1,000. Robert never got past $400 but he was still trying. You had to know an awful lot about a gazillion different topics to be on the show.

At last, Frank Farraday arrived. Mrs. Bernthal welcomed him.

"Thank you for coming, Mr. Farraday," she said. "We have been reading your books and looking forward to your visit. Children, say good morning to Mr. Farraday." She stepped back to let Mr. Farraday stand in front of the room.

"GOOD MORNING, MISTER FARRADAY," all the children said together.

Mr. Farraday laughed. "Good morning, children," he replied. "You have good wake-up voices. I'm really awake now."

Frank Farraday looked like a movie star. Robert wondered if he got his tan working out in the hot sun with wild animals. He wore a plaid shirt with the neck open, a bandanna tied around his neck, and jeans. And on his feet—Robert couldn't believe it—he had hiking boots!

Smelly Feet

Frank Farraday told the class about the books he wrote. "I always felt bad that wolves were almost extinct in this country," he said.

"Extinct?" Lester Willis called out. "Do they smell bad?" The class giggled.

"No," said the author. "Extinct means gone forever. There were almost none left in any of the states. People had killed them off. They had been exterminated."

"My dad's an exterminator," Matt Blakey said.

"Class," Mrs. Bernthal said, "please remember your manners. Raise your hand if you want to say something."

Mr. Farraday cleared his throat. Robert jumped up to pour a cup of water for him. A lot of it spilled on Mrs. Bernthal's desk. She came running with a bunch of paper towels to mop it up. Meanwhile, Mr. Farraday drank the water Robert handed him. "Thank you," he said to Robert before he continued.

"You can imagine how excited I was when I heard they were bringing wolves back to one of our big national parks. I wrote and asked if I could come out and be part of the project. Lucky for me, they said I could."

After Frank Farraday talked to the class, he answered questions. Mrs. Bernthal told the class to say thank you to Mr. Farraday, and they did, in their usual way.

"THANK YOU, MISTER FARRADAY," they said as he put his hands over his ears and laughed.

As the children were dismissed for lunch, Robert stayed behind. He gave Frank Farraday the folder he had made. Mr. Farraday looked at it and grinned. "Isn't that nice!" he said. "Thank you so much." He asked where the bathroom was, and Robert escorted him there. Robert waited outside. As they walked back to the classroom together, Robert felt his throat tighten up, but he had to say something.

"You're my favorite author in the whole world," he said.

"Thank you, Robert."

"It must be great to know so much that you can write books about it," Robert said. "You are an expert on everything."

"It's the other way around," said the author. "First I want to write about something that interests me. Then I learn about it until I become almost an expert. It's one of the neat things about being a writer. You get to explore subjects that really interest you."

"Like animals," said Robert.

"Yes, exactly."

Robert had not looked at it that way before. Books had always seemed to just be there. It was fun to know that someone like Frank Farraday had to make a book happen.

Robert looked at his watch. "The parents made a special lunch for you," Robert told Mr. Farraday. "I have to take you to the teachers' lounge. It's down the hall."

"That sounds nice. I'm starved. Lead the way."

Robert left Mr. Farraday at the teachers' lounge.

"Aren't you joining us?" Frank Farraday asked.

"Um, no," said Robert. He would have liked to, but he had to take off his boots. His feet were killing him. "I have something I have to do."

As soon as he got back to the empty classroom, Robert took off his boots. His feet felt like they were on fire. Oh, did his feet feel happy as he wiggled his toes and laughed and wiggled them some more!

He took off his socks, too. That was even better. Robert sat in Mrs. Bernthal's chair, stretching his toes. He was about to tear open a Crunchy Lunch Bar that he carried in his book bag for emergencies when the door opened.

"Mr. Farraday!" he said. "What are you doing here?" He hoped that didn't sound rude. "I mean, aren't you supposed to be having lunch?"

"Oh, yes, yes, I am, and it's wonderful. I just remembered something in here that I want to do before I forget it." He found his briefcase and opened it. Robert grabbed the Whiff O' Pine room spray that Mrs. Bernthal kept in the corner. He sprayed his feet, in case they smelled.

When Mr. Farraday turned around, he sniffed the air. "I must be homesick," he said,

"because I can almost smell the pine forests of Maine."

"You live in Maine?" asked Robert. He had never been to Maine, but he had heard about it.

"Yup," answered Mr. Farraday. "Not far from the Oceanographic Institute."

"What's that?" asked Robert.

"It's a place where scientists study the ocean. They learn how pollution affects sea animals. This summer I'm going with them to study sea turtles. That's going to be my next book. Sea turtles are disappearing, and the scientists want to know what we can do about it. So do I."

"Wow," said Robert.

Mr. Farraday handed a book to Robert. "Before I go, I want you to have this. Thanks for your help. Now I'd better get back to that lunch, or everyone will wonder what happened to me."

"Thanks," said Robert, too stunned to say anything more.

After the door closed, Robert looked at the book carefully. It was a new one, *Arctic Animals*. Inside, he read what Frank Farraday had written to him.

It was tough putting his socks and boots back on, but Robert had to do it. His job wasn't over yet. He had to stick like glue to Frank Farraday in case the author needed him for anything.

After lunch, a TV crew arrived to film Frank Farraday for the local news. The kids were buzzing with excitement. Members of the crew ran around with cameras and lights. Someone patted the sweat off the reporter's face with a tissue, while someone else dragged wires out of people's way. Other people made sure nobody stood between the reporter and the guy with the camcorder.

"Will we be on TV?" asked Lester Willis.

"I don't know," said Mrs. Bernthal.

Suddenly, the reporter held a microphone out to the author, and an incredibly bright light went on. As Frank Farraday spoke to the reporter, Robert thought about the inscription in his book and smiled. Frank Farraday, the famous author, had called Robert his friend.

Lemmings

Robert sat on his bed with his feet in a bucket of water. His mom had poured some Forbush's Foot Bath into it to help soothe his burning feet. Fuzzy was scratching in her tank. Flo and Billie were cooing at each other.

He opened his notebook. He had an idea now for his report. Across the top of a new page he wrote:

OCEAN POLLUTION

But what about ocean pollution? He didn't like it, but what would he do to fix it? It should be something about animals. As he sat staring at the words, wiggling his toes in the warm water, he heard his dad calling him.

"Robert. Your school is on the TV news! Come on down and watch."

Robert almost knocked over the bucket as he got up. He ran down the stairs with his feet still dripping. His mom and Charlie had come running, too.

A reporter was talking about Frank Farraday's visit to Robert's school. The camera zoomed in on Frank Farraday with a bunch of kids around him. For a split second, Robert saw himself at Mr. Farraday's side.

"There you are!" shouted his mom.

"Well, look at that," said his dad.

"Forsooth, Sir Rob, you're famous!" said Charlie. "Dare ye mingle with the dastardly likes of us?"

"Yeah," said Robert. It was O.K. for

Charlie to tease. He was still working on his Middle Ages project, and he talked like that, even at the dinner table. It was like eating with King Arthur, except King Arthur probably never had a buzz cut.

Finally, Robert's mom and Charlie went back to what they were doing. Robert was about to go upstairs when his dad shouted, "What's wrong with people?"

Robert stopped. He thought his dad was talking to him, but when he turned around, he saw his dad was still watching the news. A reporter asked a girl why she wore a ring in her nose. The girl squinted into the camera. "Everybody wears them," she said. "It's the fashion."

"How can anyone be so stupid?" said Robert's dad. "Nobody thinks for themselves anymore. Surely not every girl wants to put a hole in her nose and look like a pig." Robert saw the little vein in his father's neck jump.

Robert didn't think he should leave while his father was yelling about nose rings, even if it had nothing to do with him.

His dad noticed that he was still there.

"Robert, would you wear a ring in your nose if someone told you to?"

"No," said Robert. For one thing, his parents would kill him if he did. For another, how would you blow your nose? Didn't it hurt? No, he definitely would not put a ring through his nose.

"This is what I was trying to tell you about those fancy sneakers, Tiger. It's the same thing. Lemming behavior."

"What's lemming behavior?" asked Robert. He knew there was no point trying to explain any more about the sneakers.

"Lemmings are little mouselike rodents," said his father. "They follow a leader blindly and don't think for themselves. If the leader jumps into the river and drowns, the rest will follow him."

Well, that *is* kind of what happened with the sneaker snobs at school, thought Robert. If only his dad could understand that he wasn't really like that.

Robert looked down at his blistered feet. Or was he?

Bigfoot

The next morning, Robert decided he would show the sneaker snobs at school that he was no lemming. But when he tried to put his new sneakers on, he discovered he couldn't get them on his feet. His toes were still blistered and sore from the hiking boots. What could he do? He needed shoes, but they had to be big enough not to press on his toes.

Charlie had left for school. Robert sneaked into his brother's room and looked in his closet. He found a cardboard shield and a breastplate and helmet covered with aluminum foil that Charlie had made for his presentation on the Middle Ages. In the back, he found a pair of basketball sneakers. They seemed way too big, but Robert took them.

In his room, he stuffed a sock into the toe of each sneaker. Then he put on his thickest socks. He slipped on the sneakers and tied the laces as tight as he could. The shoes were still too big and slipped up and down, but at least he could get them on his feet.

Robert picked up his book bag and started for the stairs. *Thunk!* He had tripped over his own feet. He picked himself up. He had to slow down.

Therump-bump. Therump-bump. Therump-bump. He went down the stairs slowly. His dad and Charlie were already gone. His mom was finishing her coffee. He had to make

sure his mom did not see his feet or she might make him change his shoes. That would be too painful. He carried his book bag low to the ground, hoping it would hide his feet. He slid onto his chair at the table and drank his orange juice.

When his mom got up to put her cup in the dishwasher, Robert got up, too. He lifted his feet high so he wouldn't trip. At the front door, he shouted, "Bye, Mom!"

"So long, Rob," his mom called from the kitchen.

Robert carefully stepped outside and went down the two front steps.

He couldn't walk to school this way, so, once again, he got on the bus. "Hi, Robert," said Vanessa Nicolini. Luckily, she couldn't see his feet from where she sat.

"Hi," Robert answered. He found a seat halfway back in the bus and looked out the window. At Paul's corner, he called to him to get on the bus.

"So are we taking the bus all the time now?" asked Paul, sliding into the seat next to him.

"No, just this one more time. Look." Robert pointed down at his feet.

"No way!" cried Paul. "Those are not your real feet."

"They're Charlie's basketball sneakers. I had to borrow them. My feet would not go into my new sneakers."

Paul looked at him funny. "Are you sure you want to do this? How can you walk in those things?"

"Slowly, that's how," said Robert. "I have to do it. I can't go barefoot."

Paul shrugged. "O.K. If you say so."

Robert was the last one off the bus when they got to school. Everything was fine until he was almost in the classroom.

Jesse came running up to him, out of breath. "Robert, what are those ridiculous things on your feet?" He laughed so loudly that other kids turned around. They laughed, too.

"Man, look at those clown feet!"

"Hey, Bigfoot is visiting our school!"

"Robert, how did your feet grow like that?"

Robert didn't answer anyone. He just hurried inside to his seat and tried to keep his feet out of view.

By lunchtime, Robert was tired of clomping around and having everyone laugh at him. He took off Charlie's sneakers, tied them together, and slung them over his shoulder. He would just walk around in his sock feet the rest of the day.

"Robert, is something wrong?" Mrs. Bernthal asked him.

"No."

"Well, why don't you put your shoes on?"

"I can't," said Robert.

"Why not?"

"I have a foot disease."

"What kind of foot disease?" asked Mrs. Bernthal, concerned.

"Um . . . it's called . . . burning toes disease."

"Really?" said Mrs. Bernthal. "I'm sorry to hear that." She wrote something quickly on a notepad. "Here. Take this to Nurse Noonan right away."

Nurse Noonan! Robert gulped. She was as big as a bear and never smiled. Nobody knew what she did to kids who were sent to her. Nobody in Mrs. Bernthal's class had ever gone to Nurse Noonan's office.

He took the note and the pass and left the room. Nobody made a sound. When the door closed behind him, Robert felt a shiver go up his spine.

Nurse Noonan

Padding down the hall to Nurse Noonan's office, Robert could hardly breathe. What was he in for now? He never should have listened to Jesse. Who was Jesse, anyway— the fashion police? All of this happened because he'd followed the crowd, just like a lemming.

At the door to the nurse's office, he listened. There were no sounds coming from inside. Maybe she was not in! He knocked lightly.

"Come in," answered a strong voice. Robert gulped and opened the door slowly. There was a huge woman standing by the medicine cabinet staring at him. She was dressed in white pants and a white top. Her hair was white, too, like a fuzzy cap. She looked like a bear, all right. A polar bear.

"Well, and what's wrong with you?" she boomed.

Robert opened his mouth and nothing came out.

"Speak up, son. What's your trouble? Have a tummy ache? Sore throat? What is it?"

"My . . . feet." Robert stared down at his sock feet.

"Where are your shoes?" Nurse Noonan asked.

"I left them in my classroom."

Nurse Noonan had Robert sit down and take off his socks.

"Oh, my!" she said, looking at his red toes with the blisters. "What in the world did this to your feet?"

"I . . . I wore boots that were too small," he said.

Nurse Noonan stood up tall. "Tell your mother it's time to get you shoes that fit!" Her voice almost rocked Robert off the chair.

The large woman went to the medicine cabinet and took down a bottle and some cotton balls. She dabbed at Robert's toes with the medicine. His toes felt a lot better already. Nurse Noonan put Band-Aids on two toes.

"Keep your shoes off until the end of the day. You can walk around in your socks. You'll have to put your shoes on to go outside, but the Band-Aids will help. And when you get home, throw those shoes away. Do you hear me?"

"Yes, ma'am." Robert put his socks back on.

As he was leaving, he turned around. "Um . . . Nurse Noonan?"

"Yes, what is it?"

"My mother didn't know I wore those boots. She just bought me new sneakers."

Nurse Noonan pushed her glasses down her nose and looked over them. "Well, why on earth would you wear those boots, then?"

Robert didn't know how to answer her. It sounded so foolish. He just shrugged. "I don't know," he said.

"Well, I guess you won't be wearing them again. Right?"

Robert forced a weak smile. "Right." He opened the door and left.

Nurse Noonan wasn't so bad. She was huge, and her voice was scary, but she was pretty nice. And she had made his feet feel a lot better.

When Robert returned to his class-room, everyone stopped what they were doing to look at him. "He's O.K.," someone whispered.

"Yo, Robert!" called Lester Willis.

Mrs. Bernthal interrupted the class. "Robert, take your seat. We're in the middle of spelling. Open your book to page thirty-four."

Robert slid into his chair and opened his spelling book. He and Paul looked at each other. He would tell Paul on the way home about Nurse Noonan. But he wouldn't tell anyone else. Let them think whatever they wanted. Maybe it would make up for their laughing at him.

Sea Turtles

By Monday, Robert's blisters were healing. His mom had put more medicine on them. He could wear his new sneakers again. At last he could show everyone he was not a lemming.

Before Robert could sit at his table, Jesse was in his face. "So, you're back to those," said Jesse, looking at Robert's feet.

"Yup. I am," said Robert. "I like these sneakers." He slid his books onto the shelf under the table.

"I think they're nice," said Susanne Lee.

Robert looked up. The surprise on

Jesse's face almost made him laugh. There was a giggle behind Robert. It was Vanessa. She must have thought it was funny, too. And even Susanne Lee seemed to be on his side now.

Robert felt so good that he volunteered to be first when they gave their reports. His report was on sea turtles. Ever since Frank Farraday said he was going to study them this summer, Robert had tried to find out all he could about them.

Robert loved the big goofy-looking creatures. He saw a lot of pictures of them in the books he read. But the more he read about them, the more upset he became. These wonderful creatures were dying all over the place. Frank Farraday was right. They were disappearing. And it was all because of people. Pretty soon after he'd started reading about the sea turtles, Robert knew that's what his report would be about. And now he was ready.

He began. "Sea turtles live in oceans all over the world." Robert took a string out of his pocket. He taped one end of the string to Mrs. Bernthal's desk and stretched the string out, holding the other end in his hand. "That's six feet," he said. "Some sea turtles grow six feet long." Everyone stretched their necks to see. "There used to be a lot more of them, but they are dying because of things people do." He unfolded a piece of notebook paper and read:

"People steal turtle eggs and eat them.

"They put up bright lights on beaches, where turtles lay their eggs. Baby turtles leaving their nests are confused by the lights and crawl toward them instead of into the ocean, and they die.

"People make stuff out of turtle shells, like combs.

"They catch them in their nets when they fish for shrimp.

"They leave garbage on beaches that can be washed into the ocean, or they throw things off their boats. Turtles get tangled in the plastic rings that come around six-packs of soda. Or they eat plastic bags, because they look just like jellyfish floating in the water. If a turtle swallows a plastic bag, it could die."

Robert stopped for a breath.

"I don't know how to fix the whole problem. There are people studying what to do about it. But I think I know how kids can help."

"Well, good, Robert. Let's hear it," said Mrs. Bernthal.

"Never throw any garbage into the water. Not even a candy wrapper. Cut up the plastic rings from soda six-packs. And you know those balloons you buy in the park, or have at parties? With helium in them?"

"Yes, go on."

"Kids should never let them go up into the sky."

"Why not?"

"Because when they come down they could go into the ocean, and if sea turtles see them they'll think they're jellyfish, just like with plastic bags. And they'll eat them and die."

"We're not near the ocean," said Matt Blakey.

"Ah, but we have lakes and rivers, and they lead to the ocean," said Mrs. Bernthal. "Right, Robert?"

Robert nodded.

"You did an excellent job, Robert. I didn't know that about balloons," said Mrs. Bernthal. "Class, that's a very good idea." She went to the chalkboard and wrote:

NEVER LET A BALLOON FLY UP INTO THE AIR.

NEVER LET A BALLOON
FLY UP INTO THE AIR.

As Robert took his seat, Paul gave him a high-five. That's when he really knew he had done a good job.

Emily Asher spoke next about rain forests. Robert settled back in his seat.

At recess, Susanne Lee Rodgers came up to Robert and told him he'd done a great report. "I will never let a balloon go again," she promised.

Vanessa Nicolini wrote him a note with a heart on it. It said, "I hope your feet are better." Robert looked her way and smiled. Vanessa giggled.

As soon as he had stood up to Jesse, nobody said anything more about his sneakers. The sneaker snobs had finally left him alone.

That night at dinner, Robert told everyone the whole story. About the sneakers, and Frank Farraday, and Nurse Noonan, and sea turtles. Everyone had something to say.

"Tiger, you make me proud," said his father. "I'm so glad you didn't let other people make up your mind for you."

"And what an interesting idea you had about the balloons," said his mother. "Very clever."

Charlie didn't say anything. He got up and ran out of the room.

"What's wrong with Charlie?" asked Robert's dad.

"I don't know," said his mom.

Suddenly, Charlie came marching in, wearing his aluminum foil armor and carrying a sneaker on a broom handle.

"What are you doing?" said Robert.

"Here's your banner, Sir Rob," Charlie said, parading around the table. "You've won the battle against the sneaker snobs!"

Charlie made a great knight. Everyone laughed at his performance. Even Robert's feet were happy. He tapped his sneakers together under the table as he helped himself to another taco.

The Blank Wrapper

The next day, on the way to school, Paul unwrapped a piece of bubble gum and popped it in his mouth. "Hey. Listen to this," he said, reading the inside of the wrapper. "It says my name will be famous one day."

"Yeah," said Robert. "When you change your name to Sidney Famous."

It was an old joke, but they still cracked up over it.

"What about the number?" asked Robert.

There was always a fortune printed on each Bubble-oney wrapper, and sometimes a number. If there was a number you won that many dollars. All the kids were chewing Bubble-oney bubble gum like crazy trying to get a wrapper with a number on it. Robert wondered if he was a lemming for doing it, too. He hoped he wasn't because he really loved Bubble-oney gum. He just chewed a lot more of it now. He wanted to win a lot of money. Paul looked at his wrapper.

"Nope. No number. Maybe next time," he said.

Robert unwrapped his gum. "Hey! Look at this!" he said. He showed the wrapper to Paul. "There's nothing on it. Not even a fortune."

Paul looked at the wrapper. "It was probably just a mistake at the factory," he said.

Paul was probably right, but it still felt weird to Robert.

Both boys chewed furiously as they walked the rest of the way to school.

Their book bags were stuffed with Bubble-oney bubble gum. They each had to chew three pieces a day to increase their chances of winning. They had one in the morning on the walk to school, one on the way home at three o'clock, and the last one at home, after dinner. If he was a lemming, he probably wouldn't be able to plan his chewing so carefully. He would have to chew only when other people chewed. That made him feel a little better.

Trying Something New

"**C**lass, there is an epidemic of gum chewing. It will have to stop. You all look like cows when I'm speaking to you. Come up here and throw your gum in the wastebasket."

Several children walked up to drop their gum in the basket. Robert and Paul were among them.

Mrs. Bernthal was not as strict as some teachers about gum. She just never wanted to see it. "If I see it, you lose it," she once told them.

"That's better," she said, when they settled down again. "Today we are going to talk about trying something new." Mrs. Bernthal explained how that would expand their horizons.

"Have you ever avoided trying something new because you were afraid of it?"

Melissa Thurm raised her hand. "I didn't want to go on the roller coaster because I was afraid," she said. Melissa was afraid of everything.

"That's a very good example," said Mrs. Bernthal. "How about not trying something because you thought you wouldn't like it?"

Brian Hoberman raised his hand. "I thought I wouldn't like this book my godmother sent me. I put it on my bookshelf. I didn't want to read it. Then, one day, I was looking for something and found the book. I read the first few pages, and it sounded good. I read it and I liked it a lot."

"That's the point," said Mrs. Bernthal. "Trying something new widens your world. It gives you more choices, and you learn more about yourself."

Robert thought of his brother, Charlie, trying to teach him to shoot baskets in their driveway. It gave him the knowledge that he really wasn't good at sports.

"I want you to try something new," Mrs. Bernthal said. "Something you have never tried before. Each time you try something new, write down what you think of it. This is not homework. It's just something I want you to think about."

Robert liked things to stay the way they were. Change made him nervous. He'd give it a try for Mrs. Bernthal, but he didn't expect to like it at all.

Opposites

There are eight children at your birthday party. There are a dozen cupcakes. If you want to divide the cupcakes evenly among the children, how many cupcakes will each child get?

Robert kept getting different answers. Fractions made his head spin. He wished he had a real cupcake—with vanilla icing and colored sprinkles. One would be enough. Why did those kids need more than one cupcake, anyway? His mom would just put the rest away for another time.

From his room upstairs, Robert could hear the commotion as Charlie burst in the front door.

"We won! We won!" he shouted. Charlie was always winning, but this time, it meant his team would get to play in the statewide hockey championships.

"That's wonderful, Charlie," Robert heard his mom say.

"Way to go, Charlie," said his dad. He could imagine all the hugs and pats and backslaps going on downstairs.

Robert couldn't believe what opposites he and his brother were. Charlie was a real athlete and had trophies to prove it. Robert was always the last one picked for anybody's team. Even when he was forced to play dodgeball on the playground, he was always the first one hit and removed from the game.

The excitement over Charlie's good news was still in the air at dinnertime. Charlie gave them a blow-by-blow report on how his team creamed the other team. Robert never understood the fun in kids practically killing each other over one little hockey puck.

"And what about your day, Robert? What did you do?" His mom always tried to make him feel important, too. The trouble is, he never did anything like win a game for his team.

He told them about the bubble gum wrapper. Charlie thought that was hilarious.

"It proves you don't exist," he said. Robert knew he was teasing, but it still made him feel uncomfortable.

"I exist," he said.

"Of course you do, dear," said Mrs. Dorfman.

Charlie snickered as he dipped a French fry into a pool of ketchup.

"Also, Mrs. Bernthal wants us to try something new," he said. All three members of his family looked at him.

"Like what?" said his mom.

"Anything we haven't done before."

"Grow taller," said Charlie.

Robert's dad laughed at Charlie's humor. "That's an interesting idea," he said.

"What? Growing taller?" asked Charlie.

"No, Charlie. It's important to try new things. You learn more about yourself and what you can do, what you like, what you might want to do with your life."

"That's what Mrs. Bernthal said," added Robert. "But I don't know what to try." He wondered if that's how Frank Farraday decided to be a writer. Maybe his teacher told him to try something new.

"Try hockey," said Charlie, as enthusiastic about his sport as ever. "If you can get those little noodle legs of yours to hold up." He chuckled. Charlie thought he was a million laughs.

There had to be something new Robert could try that didn't involve sports. That was Charlie's specialty. Robert looked at his plate. His mom had put long, green stalks on it.

"What are these?" he asked.

"Asparagus," answered his mom.

Normally, he would just pick at them and leave them on his plate. Not this time. This was a perfect opportunity to try something new. Robert speared one of the stalks.

He brought the stalk close to his nose and smelled it. Then he licked it gently. Finally, he held his nose with his other hand and put it in his mouth, gulping it down almost without chewing. YUCCCH. It was nasty. Charlie was watching. Robert sat up straight.

"Not bad," he fibbed.

Charlie stared. "Really?"

"Really," said Robert, smiling. He picked up a chicken nugget.

Charlie went for a stalk. He put it in his

mouth, and his face turned green. He looked like he might barf.

Robert giggled. He loved it when he found ways to pay his brother back for all the teasing he took from him.

The Next Picasso

Robert could now eliminate sports and strange vegetables as new things to try. What else was there? Let's see. He already knew how to take pictures since his parents had bought him a camera last year. He knew how to keep a library in good shape from being the Class Library Monitor, and how to take care of animals from the pet service he ran.

Maybe he could paint. His best friend, Paul, was a terrific artist. Paul always had such a good time making pictures. Everyone said Paul had talent. Robert didn't know if he had talent, but he would give it a try.

He took out his paint set and paper. He dipped his brush in water and shook it until it was almost dry and the bristles came to a sort of point. Miss Valentine, the art teacher, had shown them how to do that. Then he dipped it in the blue paint.

He painted a picture of children playing on the beach. He made the sky a bright, summery blue and the sand a light tan. So far, so good. He rinsed his brush, swirling it around in the water. He shook it off and dipped the brush into the white paint, so he could put a cloud in the sky. The blue paint was still wet, so the cloud became blue, too.

The children came out a little more orange than he intended. Robert thought the big red ball they were tossing to each other was a little flat on one side and tried to make it rounder. Then the other side looked wrong, so he tried to even it out.

First he added to one side, then to the other, until the ball was twice the size it started out to be.

As he waited for the paint to dry, Robert thought of something Miss Valentine had told them once. She had showed them pictures by several famous painters. One of the artists had put two eyes on the same side of the face. She said he did that to show a new way of looking at things. His name was Picasso, and he became very famous. Miss Valentine said any one of them could become the next Picasso.

When the painting was dry, Robert thumped downstairs to show his mother. She was reading in the living room. As she studied the picture, Charlie walked by.

"Why are those men in orange suits tossing a giant radish in the air?" he asked, continuing to sweep through the room.

Robert started to answer, but his mother jumped in.

"Your composition is very good, Robert," she said, "and you are not afraid to use strong colors."

Is that good? Robert wondered. His mom was always enthusiastic about his artwork, but Robert had a feeling it wasn't a very good painting. He went upstairs and put away his paints and brushes.

He got ready for bed. "Good night, Flo. Good night, Billie," he said to his two turtle-doves. He slipped the cover over their cage so they would go to sleep.

"Good night, Fuzzy," Robert said to his pet tarantula in her little glass tank. He remembered when he first got Fuzzy. Susanne Lee Rodgers had asked him to take care of her when her cat started to look at Fuzzy as if she were a catnip toy. It was not easy trying to sleep that first night with Fuzzy in the room, but he soon got used to her and even grew to like her.

What else could he try that he had never done before? He thought about what other kids did. Kristi Mills took dancing lessons. Dancing? No way! He already knew he had two left feet. He didn't need to show every-body. Lester Willis built things. Robert didn't even know how to hold a hammer. Susanne Lee Rodgers had a pet cat. His parents didn't want pets that needed walking or could mess up the house. Vanessa Nicolini played the flute.

That's it! Music!

Tomorrow, he would ask Mrs. Gold, the music teacher, if he could learn to play a musical instrument. He had never done that before, and it was not as scary as sleeping in the same room with a tarantula. It might even be fun.

Tubby the Tuba

Mrs. Gold was flipping through a book when Robert walked into the music room.

"Good morning, Robert. You're early, aren't you?" She looked at her watch.

"Yes," Robert answered. "I want to ask you something."

"What is it?"

"Can I—I mean, may I play an instrument?"

Mrs. Gold took her glasses off and put them on her desk. "Well, it's a little late. Most of the instruments have been given out. What instrument did you want to play?" she asked.

Robert shrugged. "Anything," he replied.

Mrs. Gold walked to the back of the room. She uncovered a large shiny instrument that looked like a twisted horn. "This is all we have left."

"What is it?" asked Robert. He stared at the horn. It was huge. He hadn't thought of anything that big. Did Frank Farraday feel this funny when he saw his first wolf?

"This is a tuba," said Mrs. Gold. "It's probably too big for you."

Suddenly, Robert remembered his mom reading to him, long ago when he was little, a story called "Tubby the Tuba." She had played a CD while they read, and he heard the music that went with the story. He always loved the *OOM PUM* sound that Tubby made.

"It's not too big," he said, standing taller.

"Have you ever played an instrument before?" asked Mrs. Gold.

Robert shook his head. "No."

"Can you read music?"

"No."

"Hmmm. Well, we can try. There's an easy way to remember the names of the notes you will need," she said. She picked up a music book and opened it, pointing to the round black marks dancing across the page. "These are the notes you play. Each one is on a different line and has a name. G—B—D—F—A. You can remember 'Good Boys Deserve Fun Always.' The first letters of those words will help you remember the notes." Mrs. Gold looked at Robert. "Do you think you can remember that?"

Robert nodded. This was cool. He could remember the notes. Good Boys Deserve Fun Always. Good Boys Deserve Fun Always. He repeated the words to himself again and again.

"Now, this is how you play a G on the tuba." She showed Robert how to hold the horn and how to blow into it.

Robert tried. Nothing came out.

"You need a lot of breath to blow a note through a tuba," she said.

He tried again, harder. A sound came out, but it was more like the sound of a wounded bear than a musical instrument.

"Why don't you practice at home? I'll let you take the tuba home with you this afternoon. You can keep it there this week to see how it goes. Practice the G first. You want the note to come out smooth, not shaky."

"Thanks," said Robert.

"Come back for your instrument this afternoon. You don't want to carry it around all day."

Robert put the tuba down. "O.K.," he said. He couldn't wait.

At three o'clock, Robert ran to the music room to collect his tuba. Mrs. Gold was waiting for him. "Have fun, Robert." She had put the tuba in a battered black case that was almost bigger than Robert.

"I will. Thanks," he shouted back as he tried to run for the school bus. It was difficult, with the big black case in his arms and his book bag on his back. He usually walked home with Paul, but with the tuba to carry, he had to ride.

"I'll go with you," said Paul, when he heard about the tuba.

Lester was there when Robert and Paul got to the bus.

"Yo, Rob," said Lester. "What's THAT?"

"Hi," said Robert. "It's a tuba."

"You'll probably have to pay extra for taking up two seats."

Robert tried to smile. Even though he and Lester were sort of friends, now, Robert didn't want to say anything that could make Lester mad. Lester was too big and strong.

Jesse Meiner whistled as Robert bumped his way down the aisle to find a seat.

"What have you got there?" he yelled. "A dead body?" The other kids snickered.

"Yeah, a real fat one, all curled up," shouted Lester.

Robert went all the way to the back and set the tuba case down in the aisle. Paul sat down on the seat next to him. He opened his book bag and took out two pieces of Bubble-oney bubble gum. He handed one to Robert.

"How come you picked the tuba?" he asked.

"It was all that was left," Robert answered, peeling the wrapper off his gum.

"Awesome," said Paul.

"Yeah," said Robert. "What did you get?" He leaned over to see.

"No number," said Paul. "And my fortune says: *'Tomorrow will bring good news.'*" He crumpled his wrapper. "What's yours?"

There was no number on Robert's wrapper, either. His fortune read: *"You can do anything you set your mind to."*

Robert leaned back, seeing himself in a red uniform with gold buttons down the front, playing the biggest horn in a marching band.

"Cool," he said.

Practice

OOOOOMMMMMFFFFF.

"What was that?" Charlie came running to Robert's room and looked in.

Robert looked up from the huge instrument. "It's a G," he said.

"A what? " Charlie came closer. "What is that?" he cried. "And why does it sound so bad?"

"It's a tuba. And I have to practice," Robert answered, going back to his G note. *OOOOOOOOMP.*

Charlie covered his ears and left.

Every day, after he did his homework, Robert worked on the G note. It took a lot of wind. When he had no breath left, or his lip needed a rest, he stopped for a while. Then he started again. He played the G note over and over again until he got it nearly right. He was sure Mrs. Gold would be pleased with his progress.

On Saturday, Paul came over with his bike. "Are you ready?" he asked.

"Sure," said Robert. He was happy to take a break from blowing G notes on the tuba.

They rode over to Van Saun Park. They knew a way through the streets to avoid the main roads. They stopped at the pond and rested their bikes as they watched people feed the ducks. Paul took two pieces of bubble gum out of his pocket. He handed one to Robert. They opened them at the same time.

Neither of them had a number printed on his wrapper. Again.

"We're going broke buying this gum," said Paul.

"Yeah," said Robert. "Do you think there are ANY numbers printed on these wrappers?"

"I don't know," said Paul. "What's your fortune?"

Robert pretended to read, "Help. I'm a prisoner in a bubble gum factory."

Paul cracked up. "What does it really say?" he asked.

"It says, *'You are a person of many facets.'*"

"What's a facet?" asked Paul.

Robert shrugged. "It's what water comes out of."

"No," said Paul, "that's a faucet." He shrugged and continued reading: " *'Mighty oaks from little acorns grow.'*" Paul looked up. "Who are they calling a little acorn?" said Paul.

"Yeah. Everybody knows you're a big nut."

Laughing, they got on their bikes and rode through the park, blowing bubbles.

That night after dinner, Robert picked up the tuba and tried the G note again.

OOOOOM.

OOO-OOOOOOOOM.

OOM-OOM-OOMMMM.

OOOOOOEEEEEEOOOOOM.

After about three minutes, Charlie burst into his room. "How can a person study with that noise?"

"Sorry," said Robert, "but I have to practice." He couldn't understand why the sound of the tuba was bothering Charlie. His brother always had music playing in his headphones, even when he did his homework.

"Maybe you need to practice somewhere nobody can hear you—like out in the middle of the ocean!" Charlie threw up his hands and left. Robert heard him thump downstairs.

He blew into the mouthpiece again, harder this time. *OOOOOMMM.* He had to admit, it did sound a little like a cow mooing.

The Band

On Monday, Robert lugged the tuba to the music room.

"Hey, Robert, why did you bring the dead body back to school?" cried Lester, who passed him in the hall. "How come you didn't bury it?"

Robert just smiled and ignored Lester's remark. Mrs. Gold was happy to hear he had been practicing. He took the tuba out of its case and waited for Mrs. Gold to hear him play.

"Robert, I'd like to hear you but I've got a class coming in a couple of minutes. Can you come back this afternoon to show me? I'm sure Mrs. Bernthal won't mind."

"Sure," said Robert. He put the tuba in the back of the room where he had first seen it.

Robert felt important. The other kids would surely notice when he got a pass to go to the music room. Robert couldn't wait.

In the afternoon, when they had finished their math work, Mrs. Bernthal let Robert go to the music room.

Robert took the tuba and played the G note for Mrs. Gold. It took all his breath, but Mrs. Gold was pleased. "You must have practiced a lot," she said. "Continue to practice, Robert. Take the tuba home with you again. Learn the B note. Once you can play both the G and the B, you can come to band practice."

"Really?" It was hard to believe. He was going to play with the school band!

"Really."

"Thanks," he said.

When Robert came home with the tuba, his mother met him at the door.

"Robert. You brought the tuba home." She seemed a little surprised. "I thought you were going to leave it at school from now on."

"Mrs. Gold said I did a good job learning the G," said Robert. "Now I have to learn the B. She said I can keep it at home for another week."

Robert thought he heard a strange sound coming from his mother, but when he turned to face her, she looked O.K. He struggled upstairs with his tuba and began to practice the B.

Earplugs

OOOOOM.
OO-UR-OOO.
OOO-ROO-ROOMP.
OOOOOOOOOOMMMMMMMMM.

Ah. At last. Robert felt the note—the B—right down to his toes. It was strong, the way Mrs. Gold liked it to sound.

He was just about to play the notes again when he heard his brother's heavy footsteps thumping up the stairs. He put the tuba on his bed. No sense in having another scene with Charlie. He had practiced enough for the day. Besides, he was hungry. Dinner should be ready soon. He went downstairs to check it out.

"Hi, Dad," he said as he passed his dad, sitting in his recliner reading the newspaper. His dad didn't answer.

"Dad?" he said a little louder. There was still no answer.

Robert went right up to him and tapped the newspaper. His father jumped.

"What? Oh, Robert! Hi, Tiger. What's up?" He took something out of his ears.

"I just said hi," said Robert.

"Oh." He smiled. "I . . . I didn't hear you," he said.

Robert went to the kitchen. His mom was slicing a tomato. He loved tomatoes. He asked if he could have the end. His mom didn't answer.

"Mom? MOM?"

She turned to him and stopped slicing.

"Yes, Robert?" She wiped her hands on a towel and took earplugs out of her ears.

Oh, that's what's going on.

"I just wanted a slice of tomato," he said. Was he driving them all crazy with his playing? His mom slid the end of the tomato across the cutting board toward him. Robert picked it up and popped it in his mouth.

Well, if he was going to play the tuba, he had to practice, didn't he? He did what he was supposed to. He went out and found something new to try. He even took the tuba that nobody else had wanted. That proved he was no lemming. So what did they expect? He had to practice. His friend, Frank Farraday, had told him that. He said to become an expert you had to really get to know your subject. Well, how could he become an expert on the tuba if he didn't practice?

Robert felt more determined than ever. Someday they would realize it was worth it. They would see him march, wearing his red uniform with the gold buttons, playing his tuba. They would be so proud!

Sour Note

It was Assembly Day. Robert had practiced enough to join the school band. He had only two notes to play, but they were good, strong notes. Near the end of the second page of music, he had to play the G and the B. He could do it if he paid attention to his cue. He had practiced every day. His lip had probably grown a new muscle.

He stopped to leave his tuba in the music room before he went to Mrs. Bernthal's class. He took the tuba out of its case and polished the shiny brass with his sleeve. Then he propped it in a corner of the room. He wanted it to be ready for him when he came back later to get it. Assembly was at nine o'clock.

Mrs. Bernthal marked the attendance and asked everyone to take out their spelling notebooks. "Matt, I saw your gum. Come up here and throw it in the wastebasket, please."

Matt Blakey got up slowly and dragged himself to the front of the room. He wrapped his gum in a scrap of paper and threw it away. Robert made extra sure he didn't chew his gum so it showed.

"Here are your new spelling words for today," said Mrs. Bernthal. "Everyone write them down, please." She wrote the words on the chalkboard, and the children copied them.

cocoon	magnet
victory	reptile
wealthy	culture
journal	prowl
absent	feather

Robert had only copied eight of them when he looked at his watch. It was five minutes to nine. Quickly, he wrote down the last two words and closed his notebook.

Mrs. Bernthal had given him and Vanessa permission to leave early to join the others in the band. "Good luck!" she whispered to them.

Vanessa had cut her hair really short. Robert almost didn't recognize her at first.

"Your hair. It's different," he said.

Vanessa's hand went up to her hair as though she wanted to be sure the rest was still there. "I got bubble gum in it for the second time, and my mom got so mad she cut it short."

"Wow!" was all Robert could think of to say. Then he added, "It looks nice."

Vanessa smiled. "Thanks," she said.

There were some older kids in the music room when they got there. Robert didn't recognize them as members of the band. They must be there to practice. Some of them snickered as he picked up the tuba. He checked to see that his pants were zipped and there was nothing trailing from his shoe, but they continued to laugh.

What was so funny? Maybe they thought he looked funny, this little kid carrying the big horn. He carried the tuba out the door, and he and Vanessa walked down the hall to the auditorium.

"Don't let them bother you," said Vanessa.

Robert looked at her. "I won't," he answered. He was glad he wasn't the only one who felt the snickering was directed at him.

"Man, look at that," he heard a fifth grader say as they passed each other in the hall. Another fifth grader smiled. You never knew about older kids. Sometimes they could be nice.

Robert had never had fifth graders even notice him before. They made him uncomfortable just a few minutes ago, but now they made him feel special, and handsome, like he was already wearing that red-and-gold uniform.

The band members were assembled in

front of the auditorium, right below the stage. Mrs. Gold gave them last-minute instructions. Robert took his place on a chair behind the others. Vanessa was near the front with her flute.

He set up his music on the stand in front of him. Even with only two notes to play, he had to follow the music the others played. Mrs. Gold explained to him that a band worked together as a team. Ha! Charlie would get a laugh out of that! Robert being on a team of any kind!

He picked up the tuba and put his mouth on the mouthpiece. Uh-oh. He still had his bubble gum in his mouth. He couldn't get up and throw it away now, so he'd have to swallow it. He gulped and swallowed three times before the gum was gone.

The first graders arrived first and filled up the front rows. Behind them sat the second graders, many of them with front teeth missing. The third and fourth grade classes came next, seating themselves right behind the second graders. Finally, the oldest kids in the school, the fifth graders, came in, taking up the back rows. Robert noticed the same bunch of boys who had been in the music room sitting together, still laughing among themselves. They sure thought something was funny.

Mrs. Gold gave the signal by holding up her baton. The children stood up. On the downbeat, the band played and the children sang the first notes of "The Star-Spangled Banner." Robert watched for his cue. He had to come in right after ". . . that our flag was still there. . . ." He got ready as the music came closer to his cue.

The voices rang out, ". . . gave proof through the night . . ." Robert took a deep breath. ". . . that our flag was still there."

In the midst of the sounds of violins, a flute, a drum, and a clarinet, came the most awful sound—like a gigantic truck chugging uphill and squealing at the same time. The singing stopped. The playing stopped. Robert, his cheeks sore from blowing his horn, sat startled, like everyone else. Then laughter rippled through the auditorium, with a few whistles coming from the back. Mrs. Gold glared at Robert as she signaled frantically for the children to finish the song.

After Assembly, the children took their instruments and went back to the music room. Mrs. Gold followed them in.

"What in the world happened, Robert?"

Robert gulped. "I don't know," he replied.

"Let's take a look at that instrument," she said. She took the tuba from Robert's arms and looked inside. Suddenly, Robert wondered if he had really swallowed his bubble gum or if he had dropped it into the tuba.

"I can't see anything," said Mrs. Gold.

Robert thought his heart would stop beating. What if his big wad of sticky bubble gum was down there? What if he had ruined the instrument? All his hard work would have been for nothing. And Mrs. Gold would never let him play the tuba again.

She reached into the horn and pulled out a crumpled paper lunch bag. Horrified, Robert watched as she reached in again and pulled out a crushed juice carton. She looked in.

"I can't see anything else," she said. "It's too curvy. But I will have to get this cleaned out." For a moment, Robert had a picture of those fifth graders in the music room that morning. So that's what was so funny! But he didn't want to be a tattletale, so he didn't say anything.

"I'm sorry, Robert." She put the tuba down. "Who knows what else is down there?" she continued. "We'll have to find something else for you to play, maybe in the new string ensemble."

Robert realized with a jolt that his tuba-playing career was over. So were his dreams of marching in a band in a red-and-gold uniform.

Walking home from school, Paul unwrapped two new pieces of bubble gum. Robert read his wrapper. No number. Again. Robert was used to that. He never won anything, except once, when he won a certificate from Mrs. Bernthal for taking care of the class library. *"Expect the unexpected,"* his fortune said. Hadn't he had enough of the unexpected already? "What's yours?" he asked Paul.

"No number. And my fortune is: *'You are a person of character.'*"

"That's true," said Robert. "You sure are a character!" He laughed at his own joke, and Paul laughed with him.

Lumpfish and
Frogs' Eyes

"**N**o more tuba?" Robert's mom said with surprise. "How come?"

Robert told her the story.

"Robert, that's terrible! Who would stuff garbage in a horn?"

Charlie yelled from the living room, "I would, if it were Robert's!"

"Charlie, go do your homework," Robert's mom said.

Charlie got up and went upstairs, snickering.

"Maybe when the tuba is fixed you can play it again." Robert imagined someone

with a huge vacuum cleaner trying to clean out the tuba. But Mrs. Gold had said she would find him a different instrument.

When Robert's dad came home, he, too, tried to comfort Robert. "Don't worry, Tiger. You'll find something else that you'll love just as much."

Robert wasn't sure about that. He had really grown to love the tuba. His dream of playing in a marching band and wearing

117

the red uniform with the gold buttons was ruined.

That night, he phoned Paul. They were having a spelling test tomorrow, and he had not had a chance to study the new words. He was playing in the band when Mrs. Bernthal went over them in class.

"You copied them down, right?" asked Paul.

"Yes," said Robert.

"Then study them. You'll be O.K." Paul always believed Robert could do whatever he set out to do.

"O.K.," he said. He went over those words until he could spell them in his sleep. It kept him from thinking about the tuba.

The next day, Robert sailed through his spelling test. For a moment, he wasn't sure if COCOON had one C in the middle or two, but he wrote it down both ways and liked the one with one C better.

It was a shock when he got his paper back. He stared at two words, PROUL and FETHER.

"Pssst, Paul," whispered Robert, across the table. "Can I see your paper?"

Paul slid his paper across to Robert. He had 100 in red at the top of the page. All of his words were correct. Robert looked for PROUL and FETHER. His stomach tightened. He saw PROWL and FEATHER instead, checked off as correct.

He opened his notebook to where he had written the spelling words. "Oh, no!" he cried. Those were the last two words he had copied. He was in a hurry to get to Assembly, and he had copied them wrong.

Robert was sitting with his head in his hands when a voice came over the PA system. It was Mr. Lipkin, the principal. "Boys and girls, the problem of bubble gum in this school has become a major disaster. From now on, if you are caught chewing bubble gum in the school building you will be sent to my office and your parents will have to come to school."

Robert sat up straight.

"If bubble gum is found on you, or even in your desk or book bag, you will be punished. We must stop this nonsense now!" The PA system clicked off.

Robert nearly fell off his chair. "Paul! We have a gazillion pieces of bubble gum in our book bags!"

"We'll get rid of it at recess," Paul said. "Bring your book bag."

The clock moved slowly, but recess finally came. Robert and Paul grabbed their book bags. Susanne Lee Rodgers saw them.

"What are you taking your book bags for? We're only going to recess."

"Um . . ." said Robert. "I have a snack in mine."

"Me, too," said Paul.

"What kind of snack?" asked Susanne Lee.

"Oh, nothing you would like," said Robert quickly. He made sure the zipper on his bag was closed.

"How do you know I wouldn't like it?" asked Susanne Lee. "What is it?"

"Lumpfish!" said Paul, just as quickly.

Robert couldn't help laughing, so he turned away.

"That's disgusting," said Susanne Lee. "What about you?" she asked Robert. "You have lumpfish, too?" She had her hands on her hips now.

"I have frogs' eyes," said Robert. "They're very nutritious." Now it was Paul who had to turn away before they gave the whole thing away.

"We have to have some every day . . ." yelled Paul, as he ran from the classroom.

". . . or we'll die!" shouted Robert, running after him.

They never looked back to see the expression on Susanne Lee's face, but Robert could imagine it. She always looked at them as though they were worms.

"Lumpfish!" said Robert, when they finally got outside. "How did you think of that?"

"I saw it on a jar once, in a fancy store."

They ran to the far end of the school yard, opened their book bags, and took out all their gum. Quickly, they ripped off the wrappers to see if they had won any money. They hadn't. They threw it all into a trash barrel.

It hurt to see all that bubble gum go to waste. It must have cost them four dollars. It would be worth it if they ever won any-thing, but it was beginning to look like that would never happen.

Like Asparagus

The next day, Mrs. Gold asked Robert to join her new group of violin students. There were seven of them learning to play the instrument. Someone had dropped out, so there was an instrument available.

Robert looked at the violin. It was O.K., but he couldn't imagine himself playing it in a marching band in a parade. He learned how to hold it and how to use the bow. He had to play the notes by holding down different strings as he pulled the bow across them.

Their first practice session made quite a racket, but nobody seemed to mind. At home, everyone would probably hate him for bringing home another noisy instrument to play. He decided to leave the violin in school and practice there, whenever he could.

In spite of his efforts, Robert just couldn't learn to love the violin. He missed the tuba, which had felt like a friend to him. The violin scratched and squeaked, making him wince with every note.

One evening Robert's mom and dad suggested they go out for pizza instead of ordering in, as they usually did.

"Can we go to Pete's?" asked Robert.

"Sure," said his mom. "We haven't been there in a while. I'm sure we'd all like to see Pepperoni."

Robert smiled. He always liked to see Pepperoni.

Pepperoni was a big yellow Labrador retriever, a dog Robert had helped to train for the Happy Valley Animal Shelter. Robert loved that dog, even though he knew he had to give him up one day, when the dog had been housebroken and learned some manners. And Pete was a great owner, because he loved dogs and ran a pizza restaurant, and Pepperoni was crazy about pizza.

When they got to the restaurant, Pete gave them a big welcome. He called for Pepperoni to come out from the back and say hello, but the dog didn't come.

"What's the matter with that dog?" he said. "Let's go see." He opened the gate and let them all go past the kitchen into a small back room. Over in a corner was a cardboard box with two adorable puppies inside on a baby blanket. Pepperoni stood over them, as though he were protecting them. Robert could have sworn Pepperoni was smiling.

"Good boy," he said, kneeling down and giving Pepperoni a big hug. "What's this? Whose puppies are these?"

Pete smiled. "You have to ask? That is the proud papa right there," he said. Pepperoni's tail *thump, thump*ed on the floor.

Robert couldn't believe it. "Where is their mother?" he asked.

"She lives in the house next-door to us," said Pete. "She's a beautiful German shepherd. She had six puppies. Her family let me take these two to work so I could show them off. All six puppies are going to need homes."

Robert's heart ached when he heard that. He picked up one pup, who was climbing on the back of the other one. He looked exactly like Pepperoni, only smaller.

Robert's parents had made it very clear about no dogs. He had been trying to break them down for years, without success. The closest he ever got was being allowed to train Pepperoni for the shelter.

Finally, Robert's family went to the dining room and sat in their favorite booth. Pepperoni had to stay in the back. While they waited for their order, Robert's dad asked about his latest "something new"—the violin.

"It's O.K.," he said. "Not like the tuba, though."

"Trying something new doesn't mean you have to like it. Sometimes it's a good way of finding out you don't like something, or it's not for you."

"Like asparagus?" asked Robert.

"Yes, like asparagus. The idea is to try as many new things as possible and make choices."

"I wanted to like the violin," Robert said. "Other kids seem to get the bow and the fingering, but I just get tangled up. I even hate the sound when I'm practicing."

Charlie started to say something, but Mrs. Dorfman glared at him and he stopped.

"The thing about music, or art, or anything creative," said Robert's mom, "is that you have to really love it to do it well. If your heart isn't in it, there's no point in persisting. Would you like to give up the violin?"

Robert didn't want to seem too eager, or they would think he hadn't given it much thought. But he had. He thought about it all the time. "Yes," he said. "I would."

"Well, O.K., then," said his mom. "Explain to Mrs. Gold just as you explained to us. I'm sure she will understand."

Robert felt the relief wash over him. "Maybe I'll change my mind about the violin someday," he said. "But I really wish I could play the tuba again. I really like it a lot." Charlie groaned.

"Right," said his mom. His dad nodded in agreement, giving Charlie a look.

After they stuffed themselves with pizza, Robert wanted to stop one more time to say good-bye to Pepperoni.

"Let's all go," said Mr. Dorfman. They walked single file to the back room.

Robert picked up the puppy that looked like Pepperoni and rubbed his cheek against his soft, silky fur. His parents watched from the doorway, whispering to each other.

"Robert . . ." said his mom. "Would you like to have that puppy for your own?"

Robert wasn't sure he heard right. He looked at his father.

"Yes, Tiger," said his father. "We've been thinking. It's time you had that dog you've always wanted. You've certainly proved yourself responsible."

Robert couldn't say anything. It was too good to be true. Not letting go of the puppy, he stood up. His brain seemed to have gone dead. But he must have heard right. He was taking the puppy home!

Pete could not have been happier. "Well, you're taking Junior home, yes?" Robert nodded, hugging the puppy. "I know this is right," said Pete, "because you did such a wonderful job with Pepperoni."

Robert's voice came back, and he said, "Thanks!" While his parents said good-bye to Pete, he hurried ahead with his puppy. He wanted to be sure they didn't change their minds.

At Last

The next morning, Saturday, Paul came over to meet the new puppy. They played with it and watched it explore Robert's room.

They opened two new pieces of bubble gum as they watched the puppy play on the floor with a squeak toy. Robert's wrapper had the number "1" on it. "Congratulations," it said. "You are a winner. Take this wrapper to the store where you purchased your bubble gum. The proprietor will give you the number of dollars printed here."

134

"One dollar!" cried Robert.

"A stinking dollar!" added Paul.

"We spent a lot more than a dollar on all the gum we bought."

The gum didn't taste so good after that. They both wrapped their wads in the wrappers and tossed them in the wastebasket.

Maybe he had been a lemming, after all. He had spent all his money and chewed until his jaw ached, because that's what all the kids were doing. How could you grow so strong that you could resist the temptation to do what others did and just think for yourself? He wished he could call Frank Farraday and ask him.

A few more minutes passed, while they watched the puppy scramble after his toy.

"Well, I guess I should go get my dollar," said Robert. "But this time I won't buy more gum. I'll get a treat for my puppy instead. Want to come?" he asked Paul.

"Sure."

"Great. You can help me think about names for the puppy on the way."

They walked off toward the store. Running along ahead at the end of a brand-new leash, on his tiny puppy legs, was, at last, Robert's very own dog.